I Have...

Marina Galasso

Order this book online at www.trafford.com
or email orders@trafford.com

Most Trafford titles are also available at major online book retailers.

 www.trafford.com

North America & international
toll-free: 844 688 6899 (USA & Canada)
fax: 812 355 4082

Our mission is to efficiently provide the world's finest, most comprehensive book publishing service, enabling every author to experience success. To find out how to publish your book, your way, and have it available worldwide, visit us online at www.trafford.com

Because of the dynamic nature of the Internet, any web addresses or links contained in this book may have changed since publication and may no longer be valid. The views expressed in this work are solely those of the author and do not necessarily reflect the views of the publisher, and the publisher hereby disclaims any responsibility for them.

Any people depicted in stock imagery provided by Getty Images are models, and such images are being used for illustrative purposes only.
Certain stock imagery © Getty Images.

ISBN: 978-1-6987-1404-2 (sc)
ISBN: 978-1-6987-1403-5 (e)

Library of Congress Control Number: 2023902216

Print information available on the last page.

Trafford rev. 10/23/2023

To all the "look at the moon" people, the walk in the rain people, the people that smile at strangers and wave at babies in the grocery line.

Keep sharing your light with the world.

Special thanks to Fort Lewis College for my degree in Art Education and their support in publishing this book my senior year. To my future students and to all the young budding artists out there. To Hannah Jacks, my digital artist guru, thank you for making my ideas come to life. To my Aunt Toni and Grandma Nina, who have nurtured my love of art from day one.

Finally, I want to thank everyone who has supported me on this journey since I was 16, with your words of encouragement, purchasing copies of my books, reading them to your children, and inviting my dreams into your homes. I am eternally grateful!

Add all three books to your library collection!

I have feet that will take me anywhere I want to go,
To new faces, and places so the things I discover will grow.

I have a heart so light it glows,
And many of my best days still to go.

I have a mind which there is no limit to,
Like an endless ocean made of blue.

Sunrises let me know there's always time for a fresh start,
And sunsets remind me that even bad days create art.

With stars to make wishes and connect the dots at night,
And mighty trees that rustle and shade me from the light.

I have mama moon hanging gracefully in the sky above,
She shows me we don't need to be full to be loved.

I have Mother Nature's song to help and guide me.
Her examples of patience and kindness show me who I want to be.

I have the love of family, some I've met along the way,
And friends that inspire me and remind me everything will be okay.

With luck on my side and dreams to dare,
Goals to create with intention and care.

I have lives to live, books to read and pages to turn,
People to meet, places to see and lessons to learn.

Not all days will be perfect, some will even be hard, but you mustn't lose sight.
Don't give up, believe in yourself, and know that you will be all right.

Yo Tengo...

Tengo pies que me llevarán a donde quiera ir,
A nuevas caras, y lugares para que las cosas que yo descubra crezcan.

Tengo un corazón tan ligero que brilla,
Y muchos de mis mejores días están aún por llegar.

Tengo una mente que no tiene límites,
Como un océano infinito hecho de azul.

Los amaneceres me hacen saber que siempre hay tiempo para comenzar de nuevo,
Y los atardeceres me recuerdan que incluso los días malos crean arte.

Con estrellas para pedir deseos y unir los puntos por la noche,
Y árboles poderosos que susurran y me dan sombra de la luz.

Tengo a mamá luna que cuelga con gracia en el cielo,
Ella me muestra que no necesitamos estar llenos para ser amados.

Tengo el canto de la Madre Naturaleza para ayudarme y guiarme.
Sus ejemplos de paciencia y bondad me muestran quién quiero ser.

Tengo el amor de la familia, y de algunos que he conocido en el camino,
Y amigos que me inspiran y me recuerdan que todo estará bien.

Con la suerte de mi lado y sueños para atreverme,
Metas para crear con intención y cuidado.

Tengo vidas que vivir, libros que leer y páginas que girar,
Gente que conocer, lugares por ver y lecciones por aprender.

No todos los días serán perfectos, algunos incluso serán duros, pero no debes perder la ilusión,
No te rindas, cree en ti, todo va a estar bien.

Translated by Gabriela Rico Alvarez

"Don't lose the child in you."

Use this space to write/draw the things in your life that you value most (don't forget to draw yourself!):

Printed in the United States
by Baker & Taylor Publisher Services